Honey

This series is for my riding friend
Shelley, who cares about all animals.

STRIPES PUBLISHING
An imprint of Magi Publications
1 The Coda Centre, 189 Munster Road, London SW6 6AW

A paperback original
First published in Great Britain in 2006

Text copyright © Jenny Oldfield, 2006
Illustrations copyright © Sharon Rentta, 2006
Cover illustration © Simon Mendez, 2006

ISBN-10: 1-84715-008-X
ISBN-13: 978-1-84715-008-0

A CIP catalogue record for this book is available from the British Library.

Printed and bound in Belgium by Proost

6 8 10 9 7 5

Honey

Tina Nolan
Illustrated by Sharon Rentta

ANIMAL MAGIC
Meet the animals

Visit our website at
www.animalmagicrescue.net

Working our
magic to match
the perfect pet
with the perfect
owner!

JESS
A 5-year-old Border collie.
She is clever, lively and loads
of fun and would love to
learn new tricks from her
new owner.

NIPPER AND TITCH
4-year-old Jack Russells who
enjoy walks and would love
to go to dog training classes.
They would like to be
adopted as a pair.

MOLLY
A 3-year-old Labrador whose
owners left her home alone
and never came back. She is
shy but friendly and needs
a loving owner.

RESCUE CENTRE
in need of a home!

OLLIE
Dumped in a car park
and left to starve, Ollie
is an adorable crossbreed
who needs a home with
caring owners.

IZZIE
A long-haired Persian
with beautiful eyes. She
needs friendly, loving
owners who will let
her live indoors.

PATIENCE
Sadly Patience's owner
couldn't keep her any
more. She'd be perfect for
a family with children.
Can you help?

KITTENS!
Two black and white,
one tabby and two brown.
They are six weeks old, and
looking for new homes in
about two weeks' time.

Chapter One

"Come here, Nipper! Titch, lie down!" Eva Harrison yelled at the two Jack Russell pups who were scampering along the river bank.

The puppies ignored her and ran on through the long grass, wagging their pointed tails. "Yip-yap! Yap-yap-yap!"

Eva groaned and dashed after them. She grabbed Nipper before he could stick his head down a rabbit hole, and then dragged Titch out of the shallow water.

"Bad dogs!" she scolded.

Her brother, Karl, stood on the bridge and grinned. "Bad dogs!" he mimicked. "Face it, Eva, you're lousy at this dog-training stuff!"

The Jack Russells wriggled and squirmed in her arms as she joined Karl. She frowned at him. "Yeah, well, we're a rescue centre, not a dog-training school. And anyway, if you're so cool at it, where's Jess right this second?"

Jess was the Border collie he was supposed to be retraining. The dog was

hyper – always jumping up and running away. Her owner had dumped her at the Animal Magic Rescue Centre and it had been Karl's idea to teach her good manners.

"Erm..." Karl looked along the river bank. "I saw her a second ago. She was down there, playing with a stick."

"Oh! Isn't that her on the golf course?" Eva asked sweetly, pointing at a black and white collie charging across the smooth greens, jumping up at golfers, and then racing on towards the rescue centre.

"Uh-oh!" Karl set off after the runaway while Eva giggled. She put her two pups on leads and followed more slowly, knowing that it was suppertime and Jess would be heading for home.

But not before the young dog had bounded off the golf course on to the main street, raided a litter-bin by the bus stop, and then rampaged through the Brookses' garden, next door to Animal Magic.

"Uh-oh!" Karl said again, as he spotted Jess digging up their neighbour's lawn.

Eva held Titch and Nipper on tight leads and ducked behind a hedge.

"Shoo!" a high voice shouted. "Get away, you bad dog!"

"Oh no, that's Annie's mum," Eva murmured to Nipper and Titch, who strained at their leads, desperate to chase after Jess. "Mrs Brooks is going to be in a major bad mood over this!"

Karl dashed through the gate to catch Jess. "Heel, Jess!" he shouted, but to no effect. The collie stopped digging and ran off. She trampled through Mrs Brooks's bed of bright red tulips.

"Uh-oh!" Eva reported the latest. "Now Jess has wrecked her flowers!"

Fed up with waiting, Titch and Nipper began to yap.

"Sshh!" Eva warned, while Karl dived after Jess and chased her through Mrs Brooks's roses.

Just then, as Eva waited with the terriers on the pavement outside the Brookses' garden, her dad drove up on his way home from work in his van. He leaned out of the window. "Trouble?" he asked.

Eva nodded, pushing her heavy fringe back from her hot face. "Jess ran away!" she explained, struggling to hold the Jack Russells back.

"Come on, follow the van," Mark Harrison said quickly. "I'll park up then come back here to sort things out."

Quick as a flash, Eva did as she was told. "See!" she said to Nipper and Titch, as her dad eased the van in through the gates of the rescue centre. "That's what happens when you dig holes in lawns!"

Titch wagged his tail. Nipper wriggled between her legs.

"People don't like it!" Eva explained. "They so-o-o-o don't like it, do they, Dad?"

"So?" Heidi Harrison asked Karl as they all sat down to supper. "How did Linda react when you called to say sorry?"

"She went on about her flowers," Karl mumbled with his mouth full. "She said I'll have to pay for new ones."

"Hmm." Heidi was used to complaints from next door. Ever since she and Mark had set up Animal Magic, Linda and Jason

Brooks hadn't had a good word to say about it because they said it brought down the tone of the neighbourhood. "Anyone would think Jess had committed a major crime, the way Linda's behaving!" she sighed.

"Yeah, Jess only dug a hole in her stupid lawn!" Karl sulked.

His dad shook his head. "Listen, this is one more thing for Linda to add to her list," he warned. "You know what she thinks of Animal Magic – she'd love to have this place closed down!"

The rescue centre had only been open a year. Heidi was a vet and it had been her idea to rescue stray dogs and take in cats and other pets which had been neglected. She and Mark had found an old farm on the outskirts of Okeham and they'd transformed it into a refuge for animals.

It had been a lot of work, but now they had a cattery and kennels, plus a third outbuilding to house other small animals like hamsters and rabbits. The old dairy had been turned into Heidi's clinic where she microchipped, neutered and vaccinated all new arrivals.

"They can't do that – can they?" Eva stared at her dad open mouthed. "I mean, they can't close us down. What would happen to all the animals?"

"Don't worry, Eva," said Mum. "Linda Brooks is pretty much a lone voice. Most people in Okeham like what we're doing. You can tell that by our visitor numbers and the hits we get on the website."

"That's right," Karl said, pushing away his empty plate. "Anyway, I'm off upstairs." He was still in a mood over having to say sorry to Linda.

"'Thanks for a lovely meal, Mum!'" his dad reminded Karl with a grin. "Are you working on the website?"

Karl nodded and shuffled towards the stairs. "I'm setting up an Animal Magic forum, so people can email each other about how cool we are."

"Can I help?" Eva jumped up to follow.

"Nope," he muttered, disappearing up to his room.

So Eva shrugged and went to feed the

animals instead, running across the yard to the cowshed that had been converted into kennels. She was greeted by a chorus of woofs and yaps.

"Hi, Titch! Down, Nipper!" she grinned, giving them their dishes of food and watching them gobble hungrily.

Each dog had a special diet for its size and age, worked out by Eva's mum. Eva went along the row, opening each kennel door and saying hello to runaway Jess, then to Molly, a three-year-old Labrador whose owners had left her home alone and never come back. Next was Ollie, the little black cross-breed who had been abandoned in a car park and left to starve. For each dog there was a sad story to tell.

"But with a happy ending!" Eva sighed, watching them feed. "You're here now!"

Molly came up, asking to be stroked. Ollie joined her. Soon Eva was surrounded by happy, snuffling, tail-wagging dogs.

"We'll look after you," she promised, giving them each a hug. "We'll find new owners and you'll live happily ever after!"

Chapter Two

"Can I see the kittens?" Annie Brooks asked.

It was early Saturday morning and Eva had answered the door before anyone else was up. She dragged Annie into the house.

"Have you any idea what time it is?" Eva demanded. Even though Annie was her best friend from school, she hadn't expected to see her this early.

Annie nodded. "I crept out before Mum and Dad were up."

"Is your mum still mad at us?"

Annie nodded. "I had to sneak out. I'm dying to see those kittens your dad found."

Eva smiled at her friend. She'd told Annie about her dad's latest rescue the day before, during school playtime. Her dad had found the kittens on Thursday night, in the car park behind the supermarket. "Come and help me give them some milk."

Quickly, the girls scooted across the yard, ignoring the yelps and barks from the kennels and heading for the adjoining cattery instead. They went in and closed the door. "Is anyone around?" Eva called.

A tall, sleepy-looking figure emerged from the small office.

"Hi, Joel." Eva smiled. "Have you been here all night?"

Joel Allerton nodded. He was the main Animal Magic assistant, and that meant sometimes working nights. "I've got the weekend off, so I've been trying to get up to date with some paperwork before I leave. It's been quiet all night, thank heavens."

"Where are the new kittens?" Annie asked excitedly.

Joel took Eva and Annie to a quiet corner where the kittens were kept in a basket under a special heat lamp. Then he went off to prepare some warm milk.

Annie peered into the basket, which was lined with a red blanket and contained five adorable kittens – two black and white, one tabby, and two brown. They stared back with big, bright eyes, licking their lips with tiny, pink tongues and miaowing hungrily.

"Aah!" Annie cried, carried away with delight. "They're gorgeous!"

Eva reached in and gently lifted the nearest kitten out of the basket. The helpless tabby nestled in her hand, licking her thumb with its rough tongue.

"Ohhh!" Annie cried, reaching out to take it. "So-o-o cute!"

Joel came back and showed her how to offer milk to the kitten from a small plastic dropper while Eva got on with feeding the rest.

"Here, little kitty!" Eva murmured, smiling as each hungry kitten opened its mouth and drank. "How could anyone put you in a box and dump you?" she wondered.

"Yes, how could they?" Annie echoed, thrilled by the whole thing.

Eva fed four kittens and smiled as she

watched them playing. She grinned at Annie, who was still feeding the little tabby. "I can see I'll have to drag you away!" she said.

Eva lifted the sleepy kitten from Annie's lap and placed it in the basket.

"See you on Monday!" she called to Joel, whose eyelids were seriously drooping as Heidi came in to take over.

"There you are, Eva. And Annie, too. Eva, your dad wants you to walk the Jack Russells," her mum told her. "But have breakfast first."

"I'd better go, before Mum misses me," Annie decided.

She and Eva said goodbye in the yard, and then Eva wandered out of the front gate, along the street and down the lane at the far side of their house. She went in through a side gate, and was about to go back and walk the dogs when she happened to glance down and see a battered cardboard box placed carefully to one side of the lane. The box was taped shut. It had air holes punched in the lid and one word scrawled in black felt-tip.

Eva's heart thudded and missed a beat. She crouched down and read the name: "Honey".

Each time it happened, Eva felt sick. *How could you? So cruel! So unfair!* These were the thoughts that hammered at her head every single time someone dumped their pet at Animal Magic.

But then she clicked into action, pulling back the tape and opening the lid a fraction. She peered inside.

A pair of dark brown eyes stared back at her.

"Don't be scared," Eva said softly. She could hear a tiny whimper and made out a small, cream shape. She pulled back the cardboard flaps and reached inside, lifting out a shivering, frightened puppy.

Eva's heart melted. "Ah!" she exclaimed, nestling the puppy against her. "You're beautiful! Ssh, don't be scared!"

"What have you got there?" Karl appeared. He'd been watching from his bedroom window and come to investigate.

Eva showed him the pup. "Golden retriever," Karl noted, reaching out to stroke the puppy's head. "Probably about twelve weeks old." He didn't let on to his kid sister that he too wanted to cuddle and comfort the puppy.

He picked up the box and examined it for clues. "Have you looked to see if there's a collar?"

Eva checked around Honey's neck. "Nope. Is there an address on the box?"

"No, but I know where it came from." Karl frowned as he read the print on the sides of the box.

Too busy with the latest arrival to take much notice, Eva carried the puppy towards the surgery. Her mum came out to meet her, taking Honey inside and straight away putting her through the usual checks and tests.

"She's not microchipped," Heidi muttered, examining Honey under the bright lights of the surgery. "And I guess she's not vaccinated, either. She's slightly dehydrated, but other than that she seems OK. Eva, could you mix up a drop of glucose solution in this dish? That's great, thanks. Look at her gulp that down!"

Eva nodded. She'd begun to relax. *I wonder where she came from?* she thought. At least the owner cared enough to dump her somewhere where they knew she'd be looked after. "I bet she's hungry," she said to her mum.

"Yes, you fetch her some puppy-mix while I give her a jab," Heidi agreed. As Eva hurried off, she prepared a needle for the injection. "This might hurt a tiny bit," she told Honey, as if the puppy understood every word. "But it will stop you from getting any nasty bugs and it'll soon be over."

Eva heard a high-pitched yelp. *Aah!* she thought, fetching the food quickly.

Before long, the creamy bundle of fur had her nose deep in the dish and was happily chomping her breakfast.

"Good!" Heidi gave a satisfied nod.

"Totally cool!" Eva agreed. She was already looking forward to taking Honey to meet the other rescue dogs – Jess, Molly, Nipper, Titch, Ollie and the rest. Soon she would have a nice warm bed and friends to play with. She and Karl would put Honey's picture and details on to the Animal Magic website and they'd find a new owner for her. "You're so cute you'll be snapped up!" she murmured in the pup's ear.

Honey gobbled greedily.

"Especially with those big brown eyes..."

Honey licked every last scrap from the dish.

"You're cuddly and soft... In fact, you're totally adorable!"

Chapter Three

"Why do we have to go to see Grandad?" Eva complained.

She sat next to Karl in the cab of her dad's yellow van as they drove along the country lanes. She'd rather have been back at Animal Magic, playing with the kittens, walking the dogs, or feeding the small rescue animals such as Snowy, the gorgeous white rabbit.

"Because!" Karl said.

"But why?" she insisted.

Karl sighed. "I showed you the box, didn't I? The one Honey was dumped in. You read the name on the side."

"So?" Eva didn't see the point of following up any of the clues to Honey's owners that Karl had found. "She's been dumped, remember. That means her owner doesn't want her."

"It said, 'Gro-well Garden Centre'," Karl reminded her. "Grandad uses these boxes to pack the plants he sells."

"Yeah, so?" Eva groaned. Karl thought he was Mr Super-Detective, but with him, two and two usually made five!

Only, when she thought about it, this time Karl was probably right. After all, the box was a possible clue and their grandad, Jimmy Harrison, did run Gro-well Garden Centre.

"Plus, there's a date on the box, showing

when it was delivered," Karl insisted, pointing to the evidence which rested on his knees. "Grandad can check it."

"So?"

"So maybe we can work out who dumped Honey! Like, stop being a total dummy, Eva!"

"I know that, *dummy*! But why do we need to know?" Finding Honey's cruel owner was the last thing she wanted to do. "Why don't we just advertise on our website and find her someone nice and kind – someone who deserves to have her?"

"Hey, you two, give it a rest!" Mark sighed as he turned the van in through the wide gates of Gro-well Garden Centre. "Your mum and I have decided it's worth trying to find out what happened, so that's that."

He parked the van and they went to find Jimmy inside the huge glasshouse full of plants and flowers. They saw him at the till – a small man with combed-back grey hair, wearing a green waistcoat over his neat checked shirt. Jimmy spotted them and waved.

Karl, Eva and Mark waited for a gap between customers, and then Karl dashed up to the counter with the battered box. "Hi, Grandad!"

"Hey, Karl. What a nice surprise." Jimmy winked at Eva. "And how's my favourite granddaughter?"

"I'm your *only* granddaughter!" She grinned. Her grandad was always winking and joking and making her laugh.

Karl rushed on. "We need your help. Can you check the date on this box! It's one of yours, isn't it? Come on, Grandad, this is urgent!"

"Whoa!" Jimmy pleaded as Karl ducked under the counter. "Slow down. Do you want to knock me clean off my feet?"

"He's playing detective," Eva warned. She explained her brother's idea about tracking down Honey's owner. "Don't ask me why!" she added with a shrug.

"Another case for Inspector Harrison!" Jimmy joked. But he was willing to help with any information he could, asking

Mark to serve his customers while he and Karl checked the computer records.

Karl clicked the mouse, flashing through recent deliveries and sales. He soon found what he was looking for. "The date on this box is last Monday. And here's a list of sales you made that day."

"Totally amazing, Karl!" Eva muttered. "Grandad probably had hundreds of customers on Monday. It could be anyone."

But Jimmy was examining the box more closely. "No, it's bigger than the ones I generally use," he said thoughtfully. "I would pack shrubs in this rather than flowers. And there was one customer here on Monday who bought a dozen laurel bushes for a hedge she's planting at the front of her house. I made a note of her name and address, in case she wanted me to deliver any more."

"Who was it, Grandad?" Karl jumped in.

"Let's see." He checked a notebook by the side of the till. "I remember now – I used three identical boxes for the laurels, just like this one. Yes, here it is – her name is Mrs R. Penny, of 16 Beech Grove, Clifford!"

"I think *you* should keep her!" Annie murmured.

It was Saturday afternoon, and she and Eva were playing with Honey in the yard at Animal Magic. The sun shone brightly, the sky was blue.

"I wish!" Eva sighed. There were only two strict rules at the rescue centre that her mum and dad never broke. One was that no healthy animal was ever put to sleep. The other was that Eva and Karl were not allowed to keep any of the rescue pets.

"Otherwise, within a week our house would be overflowing with every furry creature that crossed our doorstep!" Mark had pointed out when Animal Magic had first opened its doors.

It was a hard rule, especially when Eva fell for a pup like Honey, who was so easy to fall in love with.

"But she's so-o-o cute!" Annie lay on a bench, letting Honey crawl all over her.

The furry pup pushed her nose under Annie's shirt collar, slipped sideways and was quickly caught by Eva.

"Why don't *you* give her a home?" Eva asked.

Annie sat up and pulled her fair hair out of Honey's reach. "Are you joking? My mum would never let a dog in the house – not in a million years!"

Eva nodded. "Yeah, how could I forget?"
The Brookses thought pets of any kind were
noisy and messy. That was partly why they
hated having Animal Magic next door.

Yet the idea of finding Honey a new home nearby was definitely tempting. "You couldn't kind of ... er ... work on your mum, could you? Y'know, persuade her that she'd soon grow to love Honey if she gave her a chance!"

Annie shook her head. She took the puppy from Eva and cuddled her tightly. "You don't know how strict my mum can be!"

Just then Linda Brooks came out into her garden and from behind the tall hedge her high voice called Annie's name.

"Oops, better go!" Annie said, giving the puppy back to Eva. "Mum doesn't know where I am, and you know she doesn't like me hanging out with you at Animal Magic."

"See you later!" Eva called as her friend sped away.

"Number 16 Beech Grove, Clifford!" Karl had made a biro note on the palm of his hand. He was in the surgery, showing his mum the evidence they'd gathered.

"Nice work," Heidi told him. She was busy combing through a grey cat's tangled coat. Izzie the long-haired Persian had been found footsore and filthy on an allotment in town.

Karl sat on the edge of the table and swung his legs. "Tell Eva that," he mumbled. "She's making up all kinds of excuses to stop us finding Honey's owner."

Heidi looked up, a slight frown line between her clear grey eyes. "Don't tell me – she's fallen in love again!"

Karl nodded. "I've been trying to tell

her that there might have been some mistake – maybe this Mrs Penny woman didn't want to get rid of the puppy, or maybe she did but now she's changed her mind and is really sorry..."

"There's no need to tell me," his mum interrupted, stroking Izzie before she placed her back in her basket. She went to the window and looked out into the yard, where Eva was playing with Honey. "It's Eva you need to convince."

"Or not!" Karl said, abruptly jumping down and heading for the kennels. The door opened to a chorus of yelps and barks. "What's it to me if Eva's gone loopy over the pup. So what's new?"

Heidi shook her head and sighed.

Karl grabbed a lead, opened Jess's kennel door and strode back into the surgery. "Tell her, will you, Mum? See if you can get it into her soppy head!"

"Tell her what?" his mum asked, still gazing thoughtfully out of the window.

Karl headed out into the yard, looking grown-up and serious. "That Dad and I are going to drive into Clifford tomorrow morning to find Mrs Penny whether Eva likes it or not!"

Chapter Four

"I don't care what Karl says," Eva told Honey early next morning. She crept close and pointed a camera at the golden-haired pup. "I'm taking your picture and putting you on our cool new website!" She and Karl really wanted the website to work. Whenever a rescue animal arrived at Animal Magic, the first thing they did was to take a picture and upload it on to the site.

Honey cocked her head to one side and

stared at the camera. She blinked at the flash.

"Sweet!" Eva grinned, popping Honey into her kennel, and then dashing back to the house. She raced upstairs to Karl's room where he sat at his computer. "Quick – we have to upload this photo!" she exclaimed.

Karl clicked on to the Animal Magic homepage. "Working Our Magic to Match the Perfect Pet with the Perfect Owner!" it said. "Who's the picture of?" he muttered.

"Honey!" Eva replied. "And it's so-o-o cute!"

"Hm." Karl clicked his mouse to bring up the new forum page, where a new message had appeared recommending the centre. "I can't put her on yet. We still have to check out her history, remember."

"Yes, but!" Eva ignored her grumpy

brother and hooked up the cable to upload the image. Whatever he said about trying to find the puppy's owner, she was dead set on getting Honey's details up there as soon as possible.

"Listen," said Karl, "Honey might not need a new home – not if we link her back up with Mrs Penny and everything works out OK."

"Yeah, but Sunday's a good day for people to log on and find a new pet!" Eva protested. "What's wrong with getting started today?"

She turned to her dad, who had just come into the room. "Dad, Karl's being bossy!"

Mark took a long look at his lively, brown-eyed daughter. He guessed what was on her mind and he knew she wouldn't want to hear what he was about to say. "I've phoned Mrs Penny and didn't get an answer," he told her quietly. "But I still think it's worth a drive into town to see what's been going on."

Eva frowned. "Mrs Penny doesn't want Honey!" she protested.

"Maybe. But, Dad, tell Eva we have to check it out just in case," Karl objected. He could think of half a dozen reasons why Honey had ended up at Animal Magic.

Their dad nodded. "Come on," he said with a sigh. "Let's get this over with!"

"Don't forget to stop off at Mrs Armitage's house to collect her cat!" Heidi reminded them as they climbed into the parcel delivery van that Mark used for work. So far there hadn't been enough money to buy a special van for Animal Magic and so they had to make do. She stooped to pick up an envelope from the mat.

Eva sat with Honey curled up on her lap. "Don't worry, we won't make you go back to Mrs Penny if you don't want to," she murmured.

The puppy made herself comfy.

"Ready?" Mark asked.

"Let's go!" Karl said, map in hand. "Beech Grove is on this side of Clifford, as we go in on Castle Road."

"I know it," his dad said. "It's in a nice part of town."

Heidi closed the door and studied the white envelope. It had been delivered by hand, addressed to Animal Magic Rescue Centre.

She opened it and glanced down at the signature. It was signed by their next-door neighbours. *Uh-oh!*

Rose Cottage
Main Street
Okeham

Dear Mr and Mrs Harrison,

We wish to inform you that we have begun an official campaign to have your rescue centre closed down.

As you know, local residents feel strongly that the noise from the kennels and the ever-growing number of animals housed in the sanctuary pose a threat to the quiet, rural nature of the village.

We are presently talking with town planners and other interested parties, as well as collecting a list of signatures from residents.

Of course, we are sorry to cause bad feeling between neighbours, but in the circumstances, we feel it cannot be avoided.

Yours sincerely,

Linda and Jason Brooks

Heidi's hand shook as she read the letter. "No way!" she murmured. "This place is our life. The animals need us. I will not let them close us down!"

"OK, we have to turn left here," Karl told his dad, looking up from his map at the rows of houses. "St James Street leads on to Castle Road."

Instead, Mark drove straight on. "I promised your mum I'd call on Mrs Armitage and pick up her cat," he reminded Karl and Eva. "She lives just down here."

Feeling tense, Eva stroked Honey and stared out of the window. "Why doesn't Mrs Armitage want her cat?" she asked, as they drew up outside a small terraced house with neat lace curtains.

"Oh, she does want to keep Patience, but the old people's home she's moving into doesn't allow cats," her dad explained.

Eva nodded. "What a shame," she said. She saw the curtains twitch, then, a few moments later, the front door opened and a frail old lady appeared.

"I'll wait here with Honey," Karl said, as Eva and her dad climbed out of the van.

"Patience is ready for you!" Mrs Armitage said, putting on a brave face, though her eyes looked red. "We've said our goodbyes!"

Inside the dim house, Eva made out a sturdy pet travel basket, and inside it a sleek ginger cat with a white face and one white paw. As her dad picked up the basket, Patience let out a loud miaow.

The sound brought fresh tears to the old lady's eyes.

"Don't worry, we'll take good care of her," Mark promised. "We're not called Animal Magic for nothing!"

"And we'll find her a lovely new home," Eva added.

Mrs Armitage dabbed at her cheeks. "I know you will," she said softly. She followed them to the door and watched them step out into the sunshine with her beloved pet. "Goodbye, Patience!"

The cat miaowed as Mark lifted her into the back of the van and swiftly drove off.

"That was so sad!" Eva sighed, taking Honey back on to her lap. The puppy wriggled and strained to see the cat in the back of the van. "This is so not a good day!"

Eva stared out of the window again as her dad pulled out into the traffic. Soon the streets grew wider, with the houses set further back from the road. They passed a park with a duck pond and came to some even grander houses behind high stone walls.

"Beech Grove!" Karl announced.

"Number 10 ... number 12 ... 14..." Mark slowed the van and pulled up outside the wide gates of number 16.

Honey began to whine and struggled to see out of the window.

"She recognizes the house!" Eva gasped. "I think she's scared!"

"Eva, calm down," her dad said. He took in the closed iron gates and curved drive leading between tall trees to a porch with stone pillars and a stained-glass door.

But Eva didn't listen. "I bet Mrs Penny is a dragon-lady!" she cried. "I bet she was cruel to Honey and told her off and smacked her if she made a mess in her posh house! That's why she kicked her out and dumped her on our doorstep. And that's why Honey is shaking now!"

Even Karl seemed to have second thoughts. "What do you think, Dad?" he asked quietly.

Mark paused. He tapped the steering wheel and clicked his tongue. "We go ahead and do what we planned," he decided at last. "You two wait here with Honey."

"Please let no one be in!" Eva breathed.

Crunch-crunch-crunch! Mark trod quickly up the gravel drive. He rang the bell and waited for the door to open.

Chapter Five

Mark rang once, twice, three times. There was no reply.

Eva and Karl watched from the van.

After a while a short, stocky figure appeared round the side of the house. The man marched right up to Mark and stood with his arms folded, his legs wide apart.

"Who's he?" Eva muttered. "He doesn't look very friendly."

"Dunno. Might be Mr Penny." Karl

shrugged. "I wish we could hear what they were saying."

They waited impatiently for their dad to come back.

At last he crunched back down the drive and climbed into the van. "That was Mrs Penny's lodger," he told them. "Not a very friendly type – he didn't even give me a chance to explain why we were here. But he says Mrs Penny has gone away for the weekend. She should be back later today."

Eva breathed a sigh of relief. At least she wouldn't have to part with Honey just yet. She hugged the puppy closer to her.

"What do we do now?" Karl asked.

"Nothing we *can* do for now," his dad replied, turning the van and heading for home. "I guess we take Honey back to Animal Magic."

Eva's first job when they got home was to carry Patience into the cattery and have her admitted.

Heidi examined the ginger cat and nodded. "She's in lovely condition," she told Eva. "Well fed, with a nice glossy coat. Mrs Armitage has taken good care of her."

Eva took a photo. "We can put her on the website straight away. We'll say she'd be perfect for a family with young children – I think she'd like that!"

Heidi nodded. "No luck with finding Honey's owner, I hear?"

Eva shook her head and quickly changed the subject. "Karl says that two people want to come and see Nipper and Titch later today. And someone from the village has phoned in to say she likes the look of Izzie from her photo on the website."

"That's good," Heidi said, as if she had something on her mind. "Listen, Eva, find your dad and ask him to come and have a word with me, would you? Maybe you and Karl could fix your own lunch?"

Eva set off with the message but forgot to deliver it when she spied her friend, Annie, through a gap in the hedge. "Hi, Annie! Do you fancy taking Honey for a walk?"

Annie was round there in a flash, dressed in a new pink top and bright white tennis shoes.

Eva looked down at her own faded shirt and frayed trainers. "How come you're always so neat?" she grinned.

Annie batted her eyelids. "Blame my super-tidy mum!" she groaned. "Come on, where's Honey's lead?"

Setting off with Honey and Jess, Annie and Eva headed for the river, where Annie muckied her tennis shoes and Jess went swimming.

"Go on, you try too!" Eva urged Honey. "It's lovely!"

The golden retriever crouched on the smooth white pebbles, reaching out one tiny paw to test the water.

"Aah!" Annie cried.

"Swim!" Eva encouraged.

Boldly, Honey waded into the shallow water. But it was cold and she soon turned and scampered back.

"Wimp!" Eva laughed, watching Annie pick up the dripping puppy. Then she spotted Jess, swimming strongly towards the far bank. Which meant only one thing! The runaway was up to her old tricks.

"Jess, come here!" Eva called.

Jess reached the bank and shook herself. She cocked her head towards Eva, decided to ignore her and looked towards the golf course.

"Uh-oh, Jess is going to get us into a heap of trouble again!" Eva groaned. What should she do? Run to the bridge or wade in after Jess? She decided to plunge in, gasping as the cold water reached her knees and then her thighs. But soon she reached the far bank and threw herself at the surprised collie. "Gotcha!" she cried, quickly putting her on the lead.

She turned to Annie and Honey. "Take the bridge!" she shouted. "I'll meet you on Main Street."

"No need to wait!" Annie said, putting Honey on the lead and heading downstream. "Go home and get dry. I'll see you later!"

"Heel!" Eva told Jess over and over.

They'd skirted round the golf course and made it to Main Street, but now Jess was pulling at the lead, eager to reach home.

Suddenly, she heard a cycle bell and Karl and his best mate, George, pulled up alongside her. "What happened to you?" Karl asked, spotting her soggy jeans and trainers.

"Hey, Karl, I'll see you later," George said, pedalling on.

"Don't ask!" she muttered at Karl. "Listen, I've got a picture of Patience for us to upload. Plus, we'd better get moving with the website profile for Honey, after what we found out this morning."

"Maybe," Karl shrugged.

"What do you mean, 'maybe'? The Pennys don't care about Honey. They dumped her because they had no one to look after her when they went away!"

For once Karl didn't argue back. "I gotta go and see what George wants," he mumbled, as his mate reappeared waving frantically. "Just don't do anything till I get back, OK!"

"OK." In any case, Eva was cold and wet. So, without waiting for Annie and Honey, she decided to head for home.

When she got there, she was surprised to see that the front yard was full of cars. Joel's Beetle was there, even though it was his weekend off. And amongst the group of people standing outside the surgery door, Eva recognized Pete Knight and Debbie Fielding, two of the volunteers who helped out at the centre. "What's up?" she asked Joel, as Jess pulled her towards the kennels.

"We've been told not to say anything. You'd better ask your mum," Joel answered with a worried look.

"Heel, Jess!" Eva pleaded. She went inside to find her mum and dad deep in conversation. "What's up?" she said again.

"Nothing," Mark said quickly, obviously covering something up.

Heidi sighed and shook her head. "Eva and Karl will find out soon enough," she argued. "It's going to be all over the village before the end of the day."

Eva swallowed hard. "What is?" she asked quietly, sensing that she was about to hear something very bad.

Her mum held out a letter. "It's Mr and Mrs Brooks," she explained. "You know they don't like having Animal Magic next door to them?"

Eva nodded. She crouched and put her arm around Jess's neck.

"The bad news is, they've started a campaign," Heidi said. "It's official. Linda and Jason Brooks want to get Animal Magic closed down!"

Chapter Six

"They can't close us down. We're a charity!" Joel said firmly, as Eva walked into the yard with her mum and dad. "We don't run Animal Magic to make money. We do it for the love of animals!"

"Of course they can't," Debbie agreed. "We've been here for over a year now, and the Brookses are the only people in Okeham who are against us!"

Eva listened anxiously. Whatever the grown-ups said, she couldn't help picturing what it would be like if the Brookses won. What would happen to Ollie and Patience, and the dozens of other unwanted pets who needed new homes? What would happen to Jess? She looked down at the mischievous collie who nuzzled close, demanding to be stroked. What would happen to little Honey?

Come to think of it, where was Honey?

Eva glanced across the yard, and then walked to the front gate to look down Main Street. How come it was taking Annie so long to walk back?

Puzzled, Eva was about to turn and go back when Karl came charging towards her on his bike. "George has heard a rumour. He's just given me some mega bad news!" he cried, screeching to a stop.

"Yeah, I know," Eva said hurriedly. "Karl, did you see Annie by any chance?"

"They want to close Animal Magic!" he cried, ignoring her question. He leaped off his bike, threw it against the gatepost and dashed inside.

Handing Jess to Joel and leaving Karl to find out the details, Eva strode on up Main Street. In the Brookses' front garden, Mr Brooks was mowing the lawn. Mrs Brooks was clipping her rose bushes.

She saw Eva and stared.

Eva felt the hate-rays. She hurried on, expecting to see Annie and Honey coming towards her any second now.

But she got all the way to the old footbridge across the river without finding them. Now she began to panic, looking this way and that, checking that they weren't on the golf course or along the river bank. "They can't just vanish!" Eva muttered, wondering uneasily what Mrs Brooks would say if she found out that her daughter had gone missing with one of Animal Magic's rescue dogs. Maybe Annie had had an accident. Or else Honey had run away!

She was on the point of dashing back home for help when she saw a small movement in the long grass growing in the shade of the stone bridge. Then she heard a sharp, high yelp.

"Honey?" Eva called, climbing carefully over some rocks.

"*Yip-yip!*" came the reply.

"Annie, are you there? It's me – Eva!" She stumbled, but eventually reached the long grass. Under the shadow of the bridge she found her friend.

Annie sat cross-legged, holding Honey in her lap. Her cheeks were streaked with tears.

Eva sat beside her. "What's wrong? Why didn't you come home?"

For a long time Annie didn't answer. "It's Honey!" she said at last.

"Is something wrong? Is she hurt?" Eva asked anxiously.

Annie shook her head and cried. "I adore her! I don't want her to go. That's why I didn't bring her back!"

It was Eva's turn to be silent, as she watched Honey snuggle up to Annie in the peaceful shade.

"Do you understand?" Annie asked.

"Yeah," Eva said softly. "Of course I do. It happens to me every time we take in a stray or a reject at Animal Magic. I always long to keep every animal we rescue!" She eyed Annie warily. "I've just heard about your mum and dad planning to close us down."

"Oh no! I guessed they were about to do this!" Annie said miserably. "They're always talking about it."

"Well, now they're really going to go ahead and do it," Eva said, realizing how hard it must be for her friend.

"I hate them. I'm going to run away!" Annie shook her head in disbelief.

"You have to," Eva argued. "Listen, it doesn't make any difference – I'll still be your friend."

Annie looked up uncertainly. "Sure?"

"Deffo!" Eva insisted. "I mean, honest! We're mates, Annie – whatever your mum and dad do!"

"You busy?" Karl asked Eva that evening. He wandered into her room, hands in pockets, trying to look casual.

A single thought had run through her head all evening. *Animal Magic has to stay open!* "Leave me alone, I'm tired!" she groaned.

"Listen – about Honey. I've been thinking."

"Da-da-de-dah!" She blocked her ears.

"It's no good – I've got to make you see sense. I mean, what if Mrs Penny isn't to blame? For instance, she could've given the box away after she'd finished with it. Or maybe…"

"Tra-lah!" Eva sang. But he was getting through to her all the same.

Karl frowned. "Right, don't listen to the facts. Go right ahead and jump to conclusions!" He went out and banged the door.

Eva sat on her bed deep in thought. OK, so Karl bossed her about, like all big brothers did. But maybe he was right this time and she was letting her feelings about Honey get in the way. There was a mystery behind this, and one that needed to be solved.

But Eva would never admit this to Karl. No way!

Instead, she sat cross-legged on her bed and made a plan.

Chapter Seven

Next day at school in Clifford, Eva let Annie in on part of her secret. "After school today I'm going somewhere special," she told her. "I can't tell you where exactly!"

Annie's grey eyes sparkled. "That's not fair. Tell me!"

"Not until after I've done it." Eva stood firm. "But if it works out, it'll mean that the Honey mystery is solved!"

The mention of Honey's name sent

Annie off into a daydream. "If … if only my mum would let me have a dog!" she sighed.

"Likewise," Eva murmured. "I'd love to have Honey for keeps!" Then she gave herself a shake. "Anyway, the point is, you don't need to wait for me after school."

"Huh?" Annie broke out of her dream world.

"Don't wait for me when school finishes!" Eva hissed across the aisle.

She tingled with excitement at the thought of what she planned to do, but she wouldn't say any more.

At the front of the room Mr Craven looked up from his desk. "Eva Harrison, stop gossiping and get on with your work!" he warned.

The morning and then the afternoon dragged by. Eva's nerves were on edge and she couldn't concentrate – all she could think about was her plan. It seemed an age, but at last the school day ended. Children poured out of the classrooms into the playground, hurrying to catch their buses. But Eva hung back.

"Get a move on or you'll miss your Okeham bus," her form teacher, Miss Jennings, told her.

"It's OK, I'm not getting the bus today," Eva replied, pulling Karl's city map out of her bag and slipping out by the side door.

Once in Cannon Street, she headed quickly uphill towards the ruined castle, a major landmark towering over the houses and shops. From there, she looked down busy Castle Road, checked the map and walked on.

Ten more minutes and she'd be there. Five more minutes ... Eva began to recognize the streets which her dad had driven through the day before. She saw the park with the duck pond and the big houses behind high stone walls.

"Beech Grove!" she said quietly, stuffing the map back into her school bag. She noticed the new bushes planted to either side of the front gate. "Mrs Penny, here I come!"

The loud trill of the doorbell made Eva jump as she stood on the steps in her school uniform, waiting for someone to come to the door. Her stomach churned, her throat felt dry.

She planned what she would say: *Why did you dump your puppy?* And if Mrs Penny's answer was good enough, Eva would go on with: *I know where she is. Do you want her back?* This was her grand plan, but now that it came to it, she wasn't sure that it was going to work.

Anyway, no one came to answer the door. Eva peered through the stained-glass panel into the empty hallway. The whole house seemed still and quiet.

She was about to give up when Mr Angry came stomping round the side of the house, like he had done the day before. "What do you want?" he demanded.

Eva gasped. The lodger's eyes were small and mean. He acted like he owned the place. "Is Mrs Penny in?" she asked in a small voice.

Ignoring the question, the lodger came closer. "Don't I know you?" he quizzed. He'd obviously seen her sitting in the van with Karl. "Didn't you come here yesterday in the yellow van?"

She took a deep breath and nodded. "My dad came to ask Mrs Penny if she'd lost her puppy."

The man blinked shiftily. "What puppy?" he asked. "The Pennys don't own a puppy."

"A golden retriever, about twelve weeks old," Eva insisted, though her legs were shaking. Why was this man so angry and scary?

He shook his head. "Nah, you made a mistake."

"Can I just check?" Eva was about to ring the bell one last time when the lodger barged between her and the door.

"Didn't you hear me? You got the wrong house. Scram!"

"Hey!" Stumbling back down the steps, Eva was forced to give in. She turned and ran down the drive and into the street.

What now? She stood on the pavement and caught her breath. She couldn't believe how the lodger had acted. She didn't like how he'd talked, and no way should he have barged in front of her like that.

"You OK?" a voice asked.

Eva spun round on the pavement to see Karl standing there.

"Don't ask!" he grinned. "I knew you were up to something – I could tell by the look you've been wearing on your face all day. Then I saw you sneaking out of the side door when school finished."

"So you followed me?"

Karl nodded. "I have to look after my kid sister," he said, "especially when she's cooked up some crazy, half-baked plan!"

Chapter Eight

"I don't believe a word that lodger guy said!" Karl said when Eva told him what had happened.

"Me neither," she agreed. "But what can we do?"

"Nothing right now. It's a pity Mrs Penny didn't come to the door." As usual, Karl stayed cool. He waited for Eva to stop shaking and calm down after her encounter with Mrs Penny's lodger.

"I don't think she's in, but we could wait

here until she gets back," Eva suggested, glancing up and down Beech Grove.

"Yeah, and what do we tell Mum and Dad?" Karl pointed out. "That we went behind their backs to find Mrs Penny and got thrown out by the lodger?"

Eva sighed. "Yeah, I agree – it doesn't sound good."

"No, we have to get the next bus home. Mum and Dad have loads on their minds without us causing more hassle."

Reluctantly, Eva and Karl set off down the broad, tree-lined street. They brushed past low-hanging branches of pink blossom, stopped to let a car drive into its driveway, and then headed on towards Castle Road.

"We can get the number 32 bus to Okeham on the corner," Karl was saying.

But Eva was only half-listening. She'd

spotted a woman and a fair-haired boy talking to an old man with a walking stick on the other side of the road. The woman was pointing to a notice taped to a lamp-post. The old man shook his head. The woman took the little boy's hand and walked on.

"Wait!" Eva called to the woman, hurrying across the road without Karl.

"Eva, come back. We'll miss the bus!" he yelled after her.

But a strong gut-feeling drew her on to the lamp-post where the notice was fixed. She reached it and began to read.

"Eva!" Karl shouted, jogging after her. He drew level and his jaw dropped. "Honey!" he gasped.

The notice showed a photo of a cute, golden-haired pup, and above its head was the word "lost" in large letters.

LOST

Honey. 3 months old.
Much loved family pet.
Please phone 609754
or contact Ruth Penny,
16 Beech Grove, Clifford

"Come on!" Eva cried, skirting round the shaky old man with the stick. She raced around the corner on to Castle Road. "Hey!" she yelled when she saw the woman and the little boy. "Wait!"

"Honey, it's me, Scott!" Ruth Penny's son picked up his puppy and hugged her tightly. He and his mum were in the kennels at Animal Magic. "Do you recognize me?"

Honey licked his hands and cuddled close. She yipped and yapped and wriggled with joy.

"Oh, Honey, I thought I'd never see you ever again!" Scott whispered as he buried his face in the puppy's soft golden fur.

His mum stood beside Heidi and Mark Harrison, smiling and sniffling at the same time. "I couldn't believe it when Eva ran up to us," she said. "We were putting notices everywhere to try and find Honey, but without Eva and Karl we wouldn't have stood a chance!"

"So what exactly happened?" Heidi wanted to know. "Who dumped Honey on our doorstep?"

"Tony Evans." Mrs Penny began to explain.

Heidi gave a puzzled frown.

But Eva was buzzing with excitement. She jumped right in. "The lodger!" she cried. "It turns out he hates dogs because they bark and they can be vicious and he says they're a pest. I mean, he really hates them!"

Mark nodded. "Like Linda next door," he muttered.

"So he waited for Mrs Penny and Scott to go away for the weekend to see Scott's dad."

"My husband's working in Scotland at present," Ruth Penny explained. "I asked Tony to take care of Honey for us. It was the first time I'd risked leaving her."

"And no one knew he had this thing about dogs, 'cos he kept quiet about it," Eva rushed on. "Anyway, he sneakily grabbed his chance on Saturday morning. He found a box in Mrs Penny's garden shed, stuffed Honey into it and drove out to Okeham, where he knew no one would recognize her. And that's how come she ended up with us!"

"Thank heavens!" Mrs Penny's smiles won through her tears. "You've all taken such good care of Honey for us!"

"That's our job," Heidi said quietly. "For as long as they let us do it."

"What do you mean?" Mrs Penny asked.

Eva's mum went on to tell Ruth Penny

about the fight they had on their hands for Animal Magic to stay open.

"Let me help!" Ruth said straight away. "I'll get people in Clifford to sign letters of support. I'll tell all my friends what a good job you do!"

"Cool!" Karl said, sticking his head around the door and shoving Annie into the room. "See!" he told her. "I said we'd found Honey's owners!"

Annie sidled in and stood next to Eva.

"I take it you'll be looking for a different lodger now?" Mark asked Ruth.

She nodded. "I've decided not to report Tony to the RSPCA, but I've already asked him to move on. Next time we'll find someone who likes pets!"

"So everything's sorted." Heidi glanced at Eva and Annie. "It's time to say goodbye."

Scott Penny handed his puppy to Eva. "Say thank you, Honey!" he murmured.

Honey nuzzled Eva's cheek. She was as soft, silky and adorable as ever. It was hard to let her go. But Eva handed the puppy to Annie. "Now you," she sighed.

Annie cuddled Honey. "Goodbye!" she whispered.

Scott's blue eyes shone as he took Honey back. The beautiful puppy wriggled and wagged her tail. Goodbye!

"And now?" Karl asked, holding the door open for Scott and his mum and watching them walk across the yard.

In the background, dogs yapped and cats miaowed.

Heidi, Mark, Eva, Karl and Annie stood shoulder to shoulder under the painted sign that read, *Animal Magic*. "Now we get on with our job," Heidi decided.

"We match the perfect pet with the perfect owner!" Karl said.

Eva grinned. "And we don't let anything get in our way!"

Look out for the next book in the series!

Charlie

The home-alone kitten

When soccer star Jake Adams cancels his appearance at Animal Magic's Open Day, Eva's determined to find out why. But when she and Karl arrive at Jake's house, all they find is his ginger kitten, Charlie, locked out and miaowing on the doorstep...